First published by Parragon in 2011

Parragon
Queen Street House
4 Queen Street
Bath BA1 1HE, UK

ISBN 978-1-4454-3020-1

Printed in China

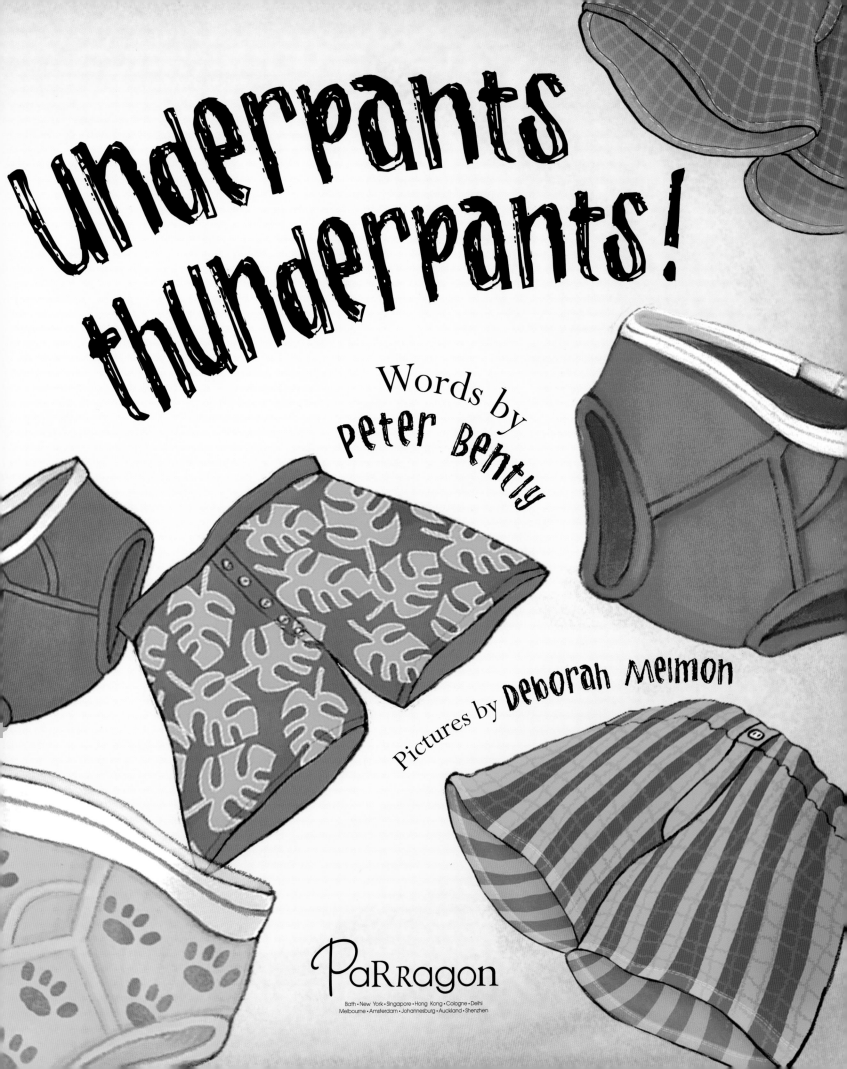

# Underpants thunderpants!

Words by
peter Bently

Pictures by Deborah Melmon

PaRragon

Bath · New York · Singapore · Hong Kong · Cologne · Delhi
Melbourne · Amsterdam · Johannesburg · Auckland · Shenzhen

One day
when the weather is
**sunny** and **fine**,
**DOG** hangs his
**underpants**
out on the line.

But **thunder** and **lightning** soon fill up the sky.

**underpants thunderpants!**

Look at them **fly!**

Over the **ocean,**
the **jungle,**
and **town**—
where will those
**undies** come
**fluttering** down?

"How odd,"
   says the submarine captain below.

   "First I saw **lightning**
           and now I see **snow!**"

Down in the **sea**
not far from the beach,
"A **giant!**
A **giant!**"
the little fish
**screech**.

Octopus **wriggles** and **jiggles** with **glee**.

"**Four** pairs of **underpants** perfect for me!"

# Underpants Plunderpants!

Just imagine that!

Roger the Pirate has got a new hat!

Safe out of sight of the **croc's** hungry eyes, Monkey's discovered a **cunning** disguise!

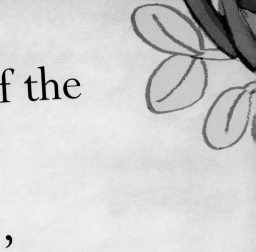

Elephant's **trunk** has been **tickled** by bees. **"Oh bother,"** he grumbles. "I'm going to **sneeze,** but I don't have a tissue. **What** shall I do?"

"A jumbo-sized
hankie!
How handy!—
ATCHOO!"

Up at the **palace,** the **King** says, "**Oh my!** **Three** pairs of **underpants** baked in a pie!"

# A two-headed alien

stares from

his **lair**...

"Underpants
wonderpants!

Now I'm
not **bare!**"

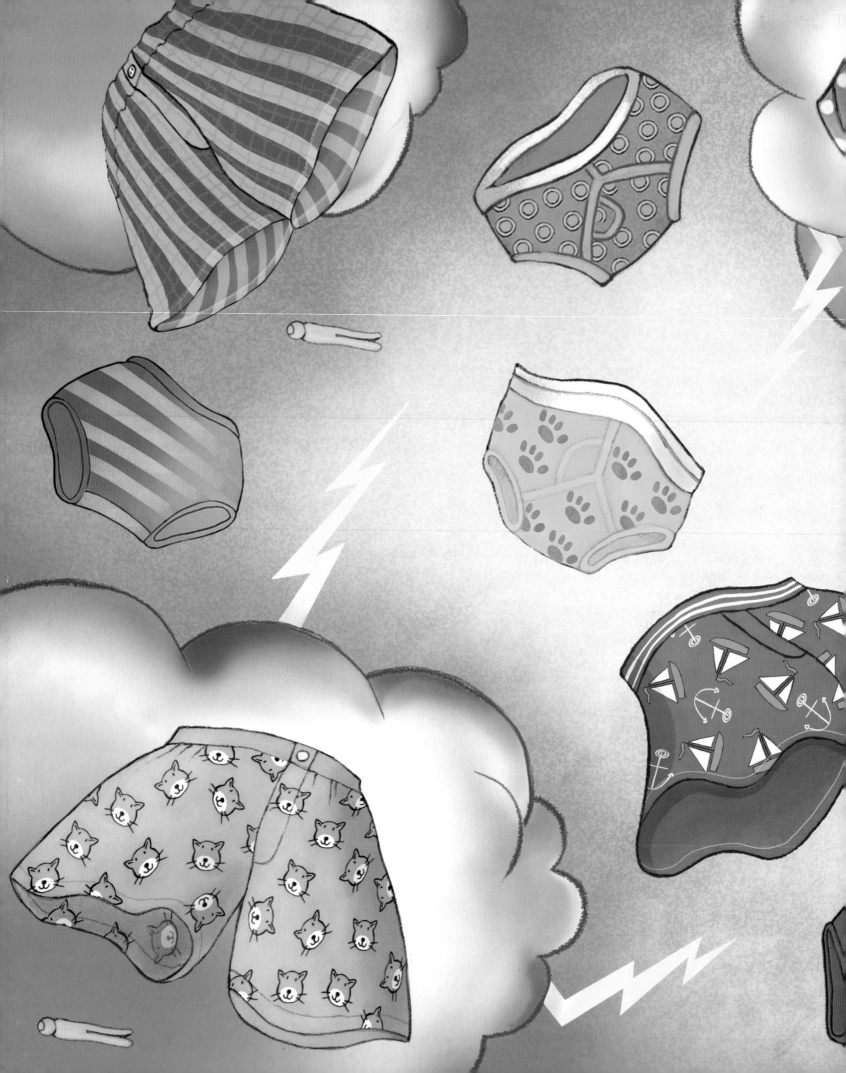